The first stars twinkled in the sky.

The driver turned out of the castle court-yard. He began his long descent down the mountain.

Suddenly, he heard screaming coming from the castle. The driver's eyes widened in fear. Never had he heard such an unearthly sound as that.

The eerie screaming filled the air as the last rays of light disappeared and darkness descended on Crittervania.

It was not the scream of a living thing.

It was the scream of the undead…

Critters of the Night...
they're here!

MERCER MAYER'S
CRITTERS OF THE NIGHT ™

The Vampire Brides

Written by
Erica Farber and J. R. Sansevere

Bullseye Books
Random House New York

40919

A BULLSEYE BOOK PUBLISHED BY RANDOM HOUSE, INC.

http://www.randomhouse.com/

Library of Congress Cataloging-in-Publication Data
Mayer, Mercer.
The vampire brides / written by Erica Farber and J. R. Sansevere.
    p. cm. — (Critters of the night)
"Bullseye books."
SUMMARY: The Vampire Brides will do whatever it takes to make Dracul Duck
their dancing partner—forever!
ISBN 0-679-87360-0
[1. Vampires—Fiction.] I. Farber, Erica. II. Sansevere, J.R. III. Title.
IV. Series.
PZ7.F22275Gr 1996
[Fic]—dc20
95-6792
RL: 2.7
Printed in the United States of America   10 9 8 7 6 5 4 3 2 1

 A BIG TUNA TRADING COMPANY, LLC/J. R. SANSEVERE BOOK

CONTENTS

Wanda   Jack   Thistle   Axel

Bones

Snake

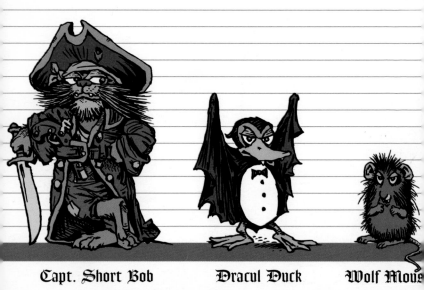

Capt. Short Bob   Dracul Duck   Wolf Mous

Toad   Frankengator   Moose Mummy

Uncle Mole   Zombie Mombie   Auntie Bell

The Castle

The driver of the cart hummed to himself as he drove along. His horse's hooves beat a pleasant *clop-clop-clop* on the winding dirt road. The hills were dotted with colorful wildflowers and overhung with leafy green trees. Crittervania was the most beautiful place the driver had ever seen.

He stopped his cart at a quaint little inn.

The driver jumped off the cart and walked inside. The inn was crowded with travelers, all laughing and talking.

"Can I offer you a cold drink, Herr?"

asked the old woman who ran the inn.

"Yes," said the driver. "I'd like some apple cider, please. And I want to double-check my directions to Castle Dracul Duck."

Suddenly, all conversation stopped. The room fell deathly silent.

"What sort of business do you have at the castle?" the old woman asked finally.

"I am supposed to pick up a crate," answered the driver.

All eyes in the room were fastened on him.

The driver took another sip of cider. He

was beginning to feel uncomfortable. He didn't know what he had said or done to upset these country folk.

The driver shrugged. Then he stood up and turned to go.

"Don't go, Herr!" screamed the old lady.

"Stay here where you will be safe!" said someone else.

"*Ordog!*" yelled another.

"*Verdolak!*" screamed a third.

The driver frowned. He knew that "*ordog*" and "*verdolak*" were old country names for a kind of creature most folks no longer believed existed. A creature known as the living dead. A creature that sucked the blood of the living under the cover of darkness.

A creature most commonly called a vampire.

The driver slowly scanned the roomful of terrified faces.

"There are no such things as vampires,"

scoffed the driver. "Besides, I am being paid a lot of money to pick up this crate."

"If you must go," said the old lady, "then hurry. Get to the castle before nightfall and then drive away as fast as you can. For at night the evil things come out. And remember—the dead travel fast."

"Good luck, Herr!" the travelers called out to him. "Be safe!"

The driver hopped back onto his cart and headed out of town. He shook his head and laughed to himself. Country people and their old wives' tales!

The afternoon sun cast stripes of yellow light along the road as the driver began the long ascent up the mountain. High atop the mountain stood Castle Dracul Duck, a dark silhouette against the blue sky.

By the time the driver got to the top of the mountain, the sun was beginning to set.

The courtyard of the castle was empty except for a large wooden crate. There was no sign of life anywhere. He called out, but no one answered. He shrugged. Better get on with it. Night was falling fast.

The driver grunted as he heaved the crate onto his cart. It was very heavy. What in the world could be inside?

As soon as the crate was loaded onto the cart, the horse whinnied and began to paw the ground.

"Easy," said the driver, patting the horse.

But the horse would not be quieted. She reared high into the air.

"Stop that!" ordered the driver. The horse stopped rearing, but continued to whinny. It was a pitiful sound.

Then the driver turned out of the

courtyard and began his long descent down the mountain.

The first stars twinkled in the dark sky. Wolves howled in the distance. Bats flew overhead. But the driver was not afraid.

Suddenly, he heard screaming coming from the castle. The driver's eyes widened in fear. He whipped the horse. Never had he heard such an unearthly sound as that.

The eerie screaming filled the air as the very last ray of light disappeared and darkness descended on Crittervania.

It was not the scream of a living thing.

It was the scream…of the undead.

Till Death Do Us Part

Deep down in the dungeon of Castle Dracul Duck, two coffin lids popped open. Two vampires sat up. They weren't just any vampires. They were vampire brides. They stared in annoyance at a third vampire bride, who was screaming at the top of her lungs.

"Stop screaming!" yelled the dark-haired bride, Sissy.

"At once!" ordered Chrissy. She covered her ears with her hands.

But Prissy would not stop.

"*Aahhh!*" screamed Prissy. Her blood-red lips were wide open, showing long pointy teeth that gleamed white in the dungeon darkness. "*Aahhhh! Aahhh!*"

Chrissy and Sissy looked at each other. They climbed out of their coffins and went over to Prissy. At the very same instant, they each slapped her on the cheek.

Prissy hiccuped once and then stopped screaming.

"You didn't have to hit me," Prissy sobbed, rubbing her cheeks.

"Yes, we did," said Chrissy.

"Why were you screaming, anyway?" asked Sissy.

"He's gone, adios, sayonara," answered Prissy. "Dracul Duck has hit the road."

"I don't believe it," said Sissy.

"Me neither," said Chrissy.

"See for yourselves," said Prissy.

Sissy and Chrissy followed Prissy up the stairs into a vast stone drawing room. In the corner was a big black coffin. The lid was open and the coffin was empty.

"Where did he go?" asked Prissy.

"And why?" asked Chrissy. "In all the hundreds of years we've lived here, he's never left us before."

Long ago, Sissy, Prissy, and Chrissy had come to an evening ball at Castle Dracul Duck. They needed a castle to call their own. So they decided to stay—forever.

After that fateful evening, there were no more balls at Castle Dracul Duck. And the brides forbade Dracul Duck to leave the castle. Their will had been law. Until now.

"Hey, look at this!" said Sissy. She held up a piece of paper she had found inside the coffin.

"What is it?" asked Prissy.

"It's a letter from those do-gooder relatives of Dracul Duck's—the Howls," said Sissy. "Get a load of this, girls."

She began to read: "Dear Great-Uncle Dracul Duck: As you know, we now live at Old Howl Hall, Great-Grandpapa Howl's old home. The place is dark and gloomy—just perfect for us. Critter Falls is a wonderful little town, which I'm sure you would enjoy. As it happens, there's a dance contest here next weekend. It would be a perfect time for you to visit, since we all know how much you love to dance. We miss you. Love, Wanda."

"How do you like that?" exclaimed Prissy. "They didn't even invite us."

"Those Howls never did like us," whined Chrissy.

"How could he dance without us!" moaned Sissy.

"After all, we are the most beautiful brides in the world," said Chrissy.

"And we can do the fango tango like no one else," said Prissy.

Prissy turned to look at the silver mirror hanging over the fireplace. "Mirror, mirror, on the wall, who's the best dancer of them all?" Prissy asked.

Suddenly, the mirror came to life and said:
*The vampire brides who number three
are the best dancers on land and sea.
But soon another will dance best of all,
in a place far away, called Critter Falls."*

At this, all three vampire brides screamed.

"Oh, no!" said Sissy.

"Who could she be?" asked Chrissy.

"We must go to Critter Falls and get

Dracul Duck!" wailed Prissy. "Before he dances with another."

"For we are the vampire brides," added Chrissy. "We are his dancing partners for life."

"Don't you mean *death?*" said Sissy.

All three brides laughed evilly.

"Dracul Duck belongs to us," concluded Prissy. "And anyone who tries to take him away will pay…"

"With her *life!*" said Sissy and Chrissy.

Moonlighting

On the outskirts of Critter Falls, high on a hill, stood Old Howl Hall, the home of the Howls. On one side was a cemetery, and on the other was a swamp.

The Howls loved their new home. And they found the town of Critter Falls simply charming. Its citizens, however, did not exactly return the Howls' feelings.

First, there was the incident with the werewolves running through town. And then there was the time all the townsfolk were turned into zombies. No one could ever pin the blame on the Howls. But everyone knew that before the Howls moved to town, things like that never happened.

"Please pass the moon lotion," Jack Howl said to his wife, Wanda.

"Of course, darling," said Wanda. She handed Jack a bottle with a skull and crossbones on it.

Jack poured green lotion into his hands and rubbed it all over himself.

Jack and Wanda Howl were moonbathing on the shores of the swamp next to Old Howl Hall. The moon was full, a round white disk in the star-filled sky.

"Thistle!" Wanda called. "Come here and put on some lotion before you get a moonburn."

"I can't," said Thistle. She was playing in the sand. "I'm in the middle of a funeral."

Thistle had dug a hole in the sand. She stuck her doll into it, head first. Then she covered the doll up, except for its feet.

"How sweet," Wanda said to Jack. "Buried Alive was *my* favorite game, too, when I was Thistle's age."

"Hmmm," said Jack, who was busy reading the *Critter Falls Tribune*. "It says here that the dance contest starts at eight o'clock tomorrow night."

"Won't Dracul Duck be pleased?" said Wanda. "What time is he coming?"

"He said it would take about a week to get here," answered Jack. "So he should arrive sometime later tonight."

"Are the brides coming?" asked Wanda.

"He didn't say," said Jack. "One can only pray not." He shuddered.

"Oh, dear, the brides," said Wanda with a sigh. "If only Dracul Duck had stood up to them long ago. Then he could regain his status as head vampire. And take back his castle. When I think of those sneaky, lazy, bossy brides—"

"Don't start, darling," said Jack. "There is nothing we can do about them. Only Dracul Duck can kick them out. He made a choice long ago. And he must live—or should I say, die—with the consequences."

Suddenly, a big explosion blasted out of Old Howl Hall. It sent Jack and Wanda flying off their lounge chairs.

"Looks like Axel's experiment was a

success," said Jack, dusting himself off.

"Our son, the mad scientist," Wanda said fondly. "What more could one ask for in a child?"

On the other side of town, a police car pulled into the parking lot of the Critter Falls Pier. The car drove slowly past the row of boats that were docked there.

The driver of the patrol car was none other than Chief Pinch, head of the Critter Falls police. With him was his right-hand man, Sergeant Pickle. They were the protectors of law and order in Critter Falls.

"It's quieter than a tomb out here," said

Sergeant Pickle. "I don't know why we have to sit here for a whole hour."

"Because that's how we cover our beat," replied Chief Pinch. He pulled a candy bar out of his pocket.

"I thought you were on a diet, Chief," said Sergeant Pickle.

"I am," said Chief Pinch. "I'm just having one tiny little piece of chocolate." Chief Pinch then shoved the entire candy bar into his mouth. "That's a mighty full moon," he mumbled, changing the subject.

Sergeant Pickle stared up at the large white moon. It seemed to be hanging right above the patrol car.

"You know what they say about the full moon?" said Sergeant Pickle. "It brings out the evil things."

"Phooey, Sergeant!" yelled Chief Pinch.

At that moment, a dense white fog engulfed the harbor. In the midst of the fog was an old cargo ship.

The ship was heading for the pier.

Closer and closer. Faster and faster it came.

Suddenly, there was a crashing sound.

"Holy smokes!" exploded Chief Pinch. He looked in his rearview mirror. The parking lot had become shrouded in white mist.

Chief Pinch and Sergeant Pickle jumped out of the car. They stared straight ahead, their mouths open in shock. The old cargo ship had crashed right through the docked boats and the pier. It had come to rest with its hull sticking halfway into the misty parking lot.

"We'd better find the captain," said Chief Pinch, "and get to the bottom of this."

Chief Pinch and Sergeant Pickle made their way toward the ship.

"Hellll-ooooo!" Chief Pinch called. He and Sergeant Pickle climbed aboard.

All was quiet. Chief Pinch shined the flashlight around. There was no one there.

"Hellll-ooooo!" Chief Pinch called again as he walked along the deck. Sergeant Pickle was right behind him.

Still, no one answered. The planks of the deck creaked eerily beneath their feet.

Chief Pinch and Sergeant Pickle walked through a steel doorway. They crept slowly down the dark hall.

"Look!" said Chief Pinch. "This must be the captain's quarters. Maybe we'll find some kind of clue in here."

Chief Pinch and Sergeant Pickle walked

into the stateroom. They stopped short and stared. The place was a mess. The bed had been torn apart, the desk drawers pulled out, and the lamp broken.

"I wonder what happened," Chief Pinch murmured.

Sergeant Pickle's eyes were wide. "It's the evil things!" he yelled. "The full moon is waking them from the dead!"

"Shut up, Sergeant!" yelled Chief Pinch. He shined the flashlight around the room again. He spotted a book lying on the floor.

Chief Pinch bent down and picked it up. "This must be the ship's log," he said. He opened the book and flipped through the pages. "That's strange," the chief muttered. "The last entry in this log is over a week ago. And it only has one word."

"What does it say?" breathed Sergeant Pickle.

"'Nosferatu,'" Chief Pinch replied.

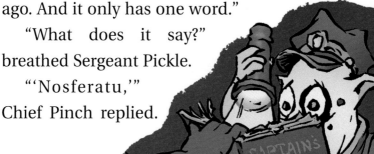

"Whatever *that* means." He held up the book, revealing the word. It was written in scrawling, wavering letters the dark red color of dried blood.

"There's an evil thing on board this ship!" gasped Sergeant Pickle.

"Get ahold of yourself this instant, Sergeant," commanded Chief Pinch sternly. He put the log into his pocket.

Suddenly, there was a loud beeping sound. Sergeant Pickle jumped.

"It's just my beeper," said Chief Pinch gruffly. "You check below. I'll go out to the car and radio headquarters."

Sergeant Pickle gulped. Then he inched his way slowly down the creaky wooden steps.

He looked around the hold. It was empty except for a big wooden crate. On the side of the crate it read: OLD HOWL HALL, CRITTER FALLS.

Sergeant Pickle tiptoed over to the crate.

The lid was gone, and the crate was open.

Sergeant Pickle's eyes almost popped out of his head as he stared at what was inside the crate. His heart pounded and a shiver ran down his spine.

It was a shiny black coffin.

At that moment, the lid of the coffin popped open. Dirt fell onto the floor of the hold as the thing in the coffin sat up.

"Aaahhh!" screamed Sergeant Pickle. He ran up the stairs as fast as he could go. "It's a vampire!"

Nosferatu

Chief Pinch pulled into the parking lot of the Crittermart. It was deserted. Chief Pinch got out of the car and headed for the store. Sergeant Pickle sat frozen in the car, staring straight ahead, his eyes wild.

"C'mon, Sergeant," called Chief Pinch. "There are no vampires out here. I promise. I'll even buy ya a Gulpy."

Sergeant Pickle didn't move.

"Get out of that car, on the double!" boomed Chief Pinch.

Slowly, the car door opened. Sergeant

Pickle followed Chief Pinch into the Crittermart. The store bell jangled.

"Good evening, Chief," said the clerk behind the counter. "I got the garlic your wife ordered. That must be *some* pizza she's making for the fair. Now, what else can I do for you fellas?"

"Sergeant Pickle will have a Gulpy," said Chief Pinch.

"What kinda Gulpy do ya want, Sergeant?" asked the clerk.

Sergeant Pickle didn't say anything.

"Give him a cherry one," said Chief Pinch.

"Coming right up," said the clerk. "You don't look so good, Sergeant."

"It was a horrible thing!" Sergeant Pickle croaked.

"What's he talking about?" asked the clerk.

"He thinks he saw some kind of red-eyed monster in a coffin," said Chief Pinch.

A strange white mist seeped into the Crittermart through the cracks in the door. Then the mist swirled into a column of shimmering white particles.

"Hmmmm," said the clerk. "Red eyes. Coffin. Sounds like a vampire to me."

"It *was* a vampire," repeated Sergeant Pickle, his eyes wide.

"Don't worry, Sergeant," said Chief Pinch. He winked at the desk clerk. "We'll just shoot this vampire with a silver bullet."

Just then, an elegant gentleman dressed in a long cape approached the counter. He stared at them with glowing red eyes.

"Silver bullets are for werewolves," said the caped gentleman.

Everyone turned in surprise.

The stranger smiled, revealing a row of pointy white teeth. Then he put a bottle of purple passion juice on the counter.

"Didn't hear ya come in," said the clerk to the gentleman, who was none other than

Dracul Duck, the Howls' great-uncle.

"He's right about the silver bullet," said Sergeant Pickle. "I saw this movie once, and this guy shot a werewolf in the foot with a silver bullet and it exploded."

Dracul Duck winced.

"That's ridiculous!" boomed Chief Pinch. "Everyone knows there are no such things as werewolves and vampires!"

Dracul Duck glared at Chief Pinch. "Nobody says that and gets away with it," he murmured to himself.

"Here's your garlic," said the clerk. He handed Chief Pinch a big bag of garlic. Then he turned to the cash register and rang up the sale.

Dracul Duck's eyes widened in horror at the sight of the garlic. He began to choke violently.

Then with a swirl of his cape, Dracul Duck disappeared.

"That'll be ten dollars and seventeen cents," said the clerk to Chief Pinch. "Hey, what happened to the dude in the cape?"

Chief Pinch shrugged. "Guess he had to run," he said.

In the Pinches' house on Main Street, Chief Pinch's wife, Agnes, was on the phone. She was on a conference call with Louise Pucker and Beatrice Plum.

Louise and Beatrice were Agnes Pinch's best friends. The three ladies were the biggest gossips in all of Critter Falls.

"I'm handling the cotton candy at the fair," said Agnes into the receiver. "Plus I'm making the biggest pizza you've ever seen."

"Well, I'm running the pie and cake table," said Louise. "On top of that, I'm baking the sweetest apple pie in the world."

"I'm not cooking anything this year," said Beatrice. "I plan to enter the dance contest."

"Go ahead and enter," said Louise, "but you'll never win. Waldo and I have won every year since we were teenagers."

"You never know," said Beatrice. "Maybe Agnes will beat you this year."

Louise and Beatrice giggled.

"You know I never dance," said Agnes, with a sniff. "And I'm not about to start now."

Suddenly, sounds of laughter came from the Pinches' kitchen. "Hold on, girls," said Agnes into the receiver. "Bruno! J.D.!" she called out. "Are you boys doing your homework?"

Bruno Pinch and his best friend, J.D., were sitting at the Pinches' kitchen table. Their schoolbooks and papers were spread all around them. But the boys were only pretending to do their homework.

"Uh-huh!" yelled Bruno. He turned another page of the comic book he was reading. It was called *The Fearless Vampire Slayers*, and it was his favorite. More than anything in the world, Bruno Pinch wanted to be a Fearless Vampire Slayer.

"Listen to this," said Bruno. He pointed to his comic book. "It says right here that vampires live in Crittervania. And whenever they leave, they usually travel under the cover of darkness in their coffins."

"Wild," said J.D.

"It also says that vampires always put dirt from their graves in their coffins," continued Bruno. "The dirt protects them."

"Weird," said J.D.

"And it also says that they can shape-shift into bats or smoky mists," said Bruno. "You know, they transform themselves like that." Bruno snapped his fingers. "And that's why they're so hard to catch."

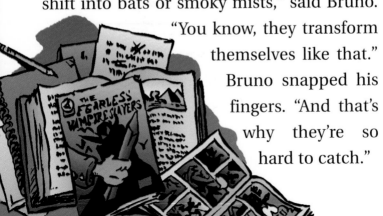

"Wow!" said J.D.

Just then, Chief Pinch and Sergeant Pickle walked into the house.

"I'm telling you, Chief, there was a vampire aboard that ship," said Sergeant Pickle. "And it was going to Old Howl Hall!"

"That's enough!" boomed Chief Pinch.

"Did someone say something about the Howls?" asked Agnes Pinch as she hung up the phone.

"An abandoned cargo ship crashed into the pier tonight," explained Chief Pinch. "And Sergeant Pickle here thinks he saw some kind of red-eyed creature in a coffin."

"Well, what about that book you found?" Sergeant Pickle reminded him. "And that strange, horrible word—*nusfusru!*"

"That doesn't mean anything," said Chief Pinch. He reached into his pocket and pulled out the ship's log. "It's just some kinda fancy foreign word. It could mean 'scrambled eggs,' for all we know."

"The word is 'nosferatu,'" said Bruno from the kitchen doorway. "And it means undead...or vampire."

Sergeant Pickle gasped. "I told you I saw a vampire!"

"That's enough of this vampire nonsense!" bellowed Chief Pinch. "You all watch too many horror movies."

Bruno and J.D. exchanged glances. A vampire in Critter Falls? It looked as if the Fearless Vampire Slayers were finally in business!

Shape Shifters

Late that night, the moon began to set. Groad, the Howls' cook and butler, headed for the Old Howl Hall cemetery. He was carrying a silver tray.

He walked up to Great-Grandpapa Howl's crypt. He pushed open the heavy stone door. Inside the crypt sat Wanda, Jack, Axel, and Thistle. They were gathered around Dracul Duck, who was lying in a long black coffin.

"Your favorite snack, sir," said Groad. "Yak's blood juice and blood pudding." He set the tray down next to Dracul Duck.

"Thank you, Groad," said Dracul Duck. He drained the bloody juice in one gulp.

"I trust you find the guest coffin comfortable," Groad said.

"It's a bit lumpy," complained Dracul Duck. "But it will have to do."

Groad rolled his eyes. Vampires! So picky!

"I'm so glad you came to visit," said Thistle. She gave Dracul Duck a big kiss.

"Yeah," agreed Axel. "We haven't seen you since we left Crittervania."

Wanda cleared her throat.

"So, Great-Uncle Dracul Duck, what about the brides?" asked Wanda.

"The brides! Are they here?" exclaimed Dracul Duck. He jumped up and glanced anxiously around the crypt.

"Why, no," said Jack. "But didn't you tell them you were coming here?"

"Uh…no…not exactly," said Dracul Duck. "I just…uh…left."

"Won't they be angry?" asked Wanda.

"So what?" said Dracul Duck, lying back down in the coffin. "Sometimes a duck has to do what a duck has to do."

The coffin lid closed with a bang.

"Well, I think it's time for bed," said Jack, yawning. "It's almost morning."

Just before dawn, three big bats flew over the town of Critter Falls.

"Aahhh!" shrieked Sissy. "The sun's rising!"

"We will burn to a crisp," moaned Chrissy, "if we are caught in the sun's evil rays."

"Stop complaining!" shouted Prissy. "Look down there! That's where the fair and dance contest are being held."

The bats swooped low. They made high-pitched shrieking sounds.

Then they flew behind some bushes. Seconds later, Sissy, Prissy, and Chrissy emerged just as the first rays of the sun began to streak the sky.

"I hate shape-shifting," announced Chrissy. "It gives me a tummy-ache."

"Me, too," agreed Sissy. "We should have traveled by boat."

"Quiet!" snapped Prissy. "We had no choice. There was not enough time to make the proper travel arrangements."

"Now what?" asked Chrissy.

"Just wait till I get my hands on that wandering duck," murmured Prissy. "I'm going to cook his goose—"

"I'm burning!" shrieked Sissy. She pointed to her arm. It was smoking.

"Me, too," screamed Chrissy, whose hair was on fire.

"Quick! In there!" shouted Prissy. She pointed to the Fun House.

The brides hurried inside. They heaved a

sigh of relief. It was pitch-dark in there.

"Where should we sleep?" asked Sissy as they wandered through the rooms.

"There," said Prissy. She pointed to a room that had been decorated to look like a cave.

"Perfect," said Sissy. "It will be just like the old days."

The vampire brides flew up to the rafters and hung upside down, like bats.

They began to snore as they fell into a deep sleep.

Vampire Slayers

Later that morning, Bruno met J.D. in front of his house. The two boys turned down Main Street and headed for Critter Falls Elementary School.

"Wait till that nosferatu guy finds out there are vampire slayers in town," bragged Bruno. "We're gonna get him."

"How are we gonna do that?" asked J.D.

"We're gonna stake him right through the heart," said Bruno.

"Cool," said J.D. "That bloodsucker doesn't stand a chance."

Just then, the bell rang. The two boys hurried into the school building.

Axel was standing at his locker. It was number thirteen. His favorite number. He was talking to his best friend, Wilbur Jenkins.

"Did your great-uncle from Crittervania come last night?" Wilbur asked Axel.

"Yep," said Axel. He took his lunchbox out of his knapsack. "You can meet him at the fair tonight. He's really cool!"

"Hey, give me that!" a voice said.

Before Axel or Wilbur could turn around, a fat hand reached out and grabbed Wilbur's lunch. The hand belonged to none other than Bruno Pinch.

"That's not yours," said Axel. "Give it back!"

A crowd of kids gathered to watch the bullies in action.

Bruno and J.D. laughed and opened Wilbur's lunchbox. Bruno pulled out a chocolate cupcake. "Critter Doodles!" he exclaimed. "My favorite!" He wolfed down the cupcake.

Bruno turned to Axel. "Now let's see what you've got," he said. And he snatched Axel's lunchbox away from him.

He groped around inside the box. Then he pulled out a bag of chocolate candies.

"Chocolate!" Bruno exclaimed. "I love chocolate."

He crammed a fistful of candies into his mouth. Then he handed some to J.D.

"Hey, these are really good!" said Bruno. "What are they?"

"Chocolate-covered spiders," said Axel.

Suddenly, Bruno and J.D. began to gag. They spit out the half-chewed chocolate-covered spiders all over the floor.

"Gross!" Bruno yelled. "I think I'm gonna hurl."

"Me, too," said J.D., gagging.

The crowd laughed at Bruno and J.D.

Bruno's face turned red. His eyes bugged out. His breath wheezed. "No one laughs at Bruno Pinch! You're gonna pay for this, jerk," Bruno yelled at Axel.

Axel looked Bruno right in the eye and said, "I'm not afraid of you."

"Yeah?" said Bruno. "Well, you should be. You and your whole creepy family. By the time I'm finished with you, you Howls are gonna be sorry you ever moved to Critter Falls!"

"We know all about the vampire that came to your house last night," added J.D.

"And the Fearless Vampire Slayers are gonna get him!" exclaimed Bruno.

Stakes and Roses

By sunset, the Critter Falls fair was in full swing. The entire village green was lit up. On one side was a big Ferris wheel and on the other was a roller coaster.

In the very center of the green was a huge striped tent. Inside the tent were the fair and game booths. There were critters everywhere.

"Do ya see him?" Bruno asked J.D. The two boys scanned the big crowd in the tent.

"How are we gonna know who the vampire is, anyway?" asked J.D.

"We'll just know," said Bruno. "He'll be pale and have red eyes and be wearin' one of those weird black capes. Hey, we better check out our equipment," he added.

"Let's go outside," said J.D. "That way nobody'll see us."

The two boys walked out of the tent and headed around to the back.

"Garlic," Bruno read aloud from his *Fearless Vampire Slayers* comic book.

J.D. pulled out two braids of garlic. "Check," said J.D.

He put one braid around his neck and handed the other to Bruno. Bruno did the same.

"Water pistols," said Bruno.

"Check," said J.D. He took out two large plastic pistols loaded with water.

"You got the rose petals?" Bruno asked.

"Check," said J.D.

He pulled out a plastic bag filled with red and pink petals. "I pulled 'em off my mom's prize roses."

"Cool," said Bruno.

He and J.D. stuffed rose petals into their pistols. Then each boy tucked his pistol into the top of his pants.

"Wait until we hit the vampire dude with this water," said Bruno with a nasty grin. "It will make him burn to a crisp."

"He'll be one sorry bloodsucker," said J.D.

"So, where are the stakes?" asked Bruno.

"You were supposed to get 'em," said J.D.

Bruno wagged his head. "Big problem," he said. "We gotta get stakes. We gotta stake the vampire dude right through the heart."

At that moment, the Howls were in their car heading to the fair.

"I can't wait to see you do the fango tango," said Jack. "You always killed the ladies with that one."

"What about the vampire slayers?" asked
Axel. "Aren't you afraid of them?"

"Certainly not," said Dracul Duck. "Garlic.
Rosewater. I've seen it all. When you've
been alive for as many centuries as I have,
you know how to handle little annoyances
like vampire slayers."

"Please be careful," begged Thistle.

Dracul Duck beamed. How he loved all
this attention!

As the Howls pulled up to the fairgrounds,
Bruno and J.D. were still looking for stakes.

"Hey, what about these?" said J.D. finally.
He pointed to the stakes that were holding
up the tent.

"Excellent!" said Bruno. He yanked two stakes out of the ground. They were nice and sharp and wooden. Just the thing!

Bruno and J.D. gave each other a thumbs-up.

"The Fearless Vampire Slayers are ready to rumble," said Bruno.

"Hey, you wanna go to the Fun House?" asked J.D.

"Cool, dude," said Bruno. The two boys headed for the Fun House. "I can't wait till we see that vampire," added Bruno. "It's gonna be lights out, bloodsucker!"

The Fango Tango

Axel, Thistle, and Wilbur were already on line at the Fun House.

"Do you think it's going to be really scary?" asked Wilbur.

Axel and Thistle grinned. "I hope so," said Axel.

Just then, Bruno and J.D. walked over. They cut ahead of Axel, Thistle, and Wilbur.

"Hey, no cutting!" said Axel.

"Watch me!" said Bruno. "Besides, the Fun House is too scary for wimps like you."

"Yeah," agreed J.D. "Only tough dudes

like us can handle the spooky stuff they got in there."

Axel frowned. He opened his mouth to tell Bruno and J.D. off. But before he could say anything, Bruno and J.D. were let into the Fun House.

In the entranceway, all was dark. Spider-webs dangled from the ceiling. Spooky music played as Bruno and J.D. pushed their way through the webs.

"String!" scoffed Bruno. "Sca-ry!"

He and J.D. laughed as they headed into the next room.

Suddenly, a skeleton lunged toward them and then disappeared into the darkness.

"Ha, ha, ha!" snorted Bruno. "This stuff is so stupid!"

"It's so fake it's not even scary," said J.D.

The boys continued through the Fun House. They stared at the glow-in-the-dark monsters painted on the walls. "Pretty lame," said Bruno.

Meanwhile, in the main tent, Dracul Duck was standing with Jack and Wanda.

"I can't wait to dance," said Dracul Duck, tapping his foot impatiently. He scanned the crowd. He had to have just the right partner to win the contest.

Suddenly, he spotted Chief Pinch. The stupid mortal in the Crittermart who didn't believe in vampires. He watched as Chief Pinch put his arm around a woman. They were standing by the cotton-candy machine.

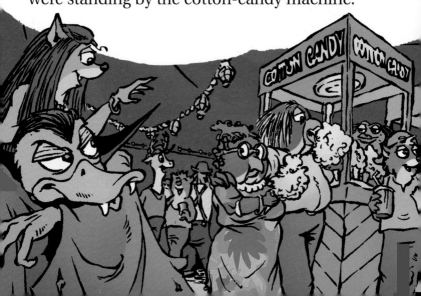

"There are Chief Pinch and Mrs. Pinch," said Wanda, following Dracul Duck's gaze. She waved at the Pinches.

"Perfect," murmured Dracul Duck. He could teach Chief Pinch a thing or two about vampires, and get a dancing partner, all in one shot.

At that moment the loud-speaker crackled.

"Ladies and gentlemen," said the bandleader. "And now the moment you've all been waiting for—the Critter Falls Dance Contest. Grab your partners, put on your dancing shoes, and let's boogie!"

Dracul Duck glided across the floor to Mrs. Pinch.

"May I have this dance?" Dracul Duck asked her.

"No, you may not!" sputtered Mrs. Pinch. "I don't dance. And I never—"

"Shhh…" whispered Dracul Duck. He smiled, revealing two sharp white fangs. His eyes glowed blood-red.

"Aaahhh!" screamed Chief Pinch. His mouth dropped open in shock as he stared at Dracul Duck.

"It's the vamp—vampire from the ship!" shouted Sergeant Pickle. He cowered behind Chief Pinch.

"Precisely!" said Dracul Duck. "May that be the very last time you dare to doubt the existence of vampires!"

Dracul Duck took Mrs. Pinch's hand. He gazed deeply into her eyes. "Now, look into my eyes, my cotton-candy queen," he commanded.

"Don't do it!" cried Chief Pinch.

But Dracul Duck's voice called out to her. "There, there…" murmured Dracul Duck. "Why fight it? Give in."

Slowly, Mrs. Pinch looked up. Before she knew it, she was staring into Dracul Duck's eyes. Bit by bit, she fell under his spell.

"Just let your feet do the talking," said Dracul Duck.

The crowd gasped as Dracul Duck glided into the middle of the dance floor with Mrs. Pinch on his arm. She smiled at the crowd. Her eyes were glassy.

"Glory be!" whispered Louise Pucker. "What's come over Agnes?"

"My word, I haven't the foggiest idea," Beatrice Plum whispered back. "And who is that dark handsome stranger?"

Back at the Fun House, Bruno and J.D. were heading into the last room, which looked like a cave.

"What's that?" J.D. asked. He pointed to three shapes hanging from the rafters.

"Just some more 'scary' monsters," Bruno sneered. "Or should I say, vampires!"

He and J.D. stared at the sleeping vampire brides. "They look pretty real," said J.D.

"Let's climb up and get a better look," said Bruno.

"Don't do it, dude," said J.D.

Bruno didn't listen. He climbed up one of the fake stalagmites. When he got to the top, he leaned closer to the brides.

"Hey, J.D.!" shouted Bruno. "These vampires are pretty cool! Check this out!" Bruno reached over and poked the vampire bride closest to him.

Prissy's eyes popped open. She let out a bloodcurdling shriek. Chrissy and Sissy bolted awake.

Bruno froze. So did J.D.

"Slayers!" shrieked Chrissy. "Descendants of Critter van Helsing!"

Sissy grabbed Bruno's hand.

"They've got stakes and garlic!" yelled Chrissy, coughing. "Get the other one!"

"We're not slayers!" Bruno lied.

"Oh, yeah? Then what are you doing with a pistol filled with rosewater?" shrieked Chrissy.

Sissy and Chrissy bared their fangs. Their eyes glowed blood-red.

"Aaahhhh!" screamed J.D. as Chrissy swooped down from the ceiling. She began to cough because of the garlic, but she came heading straight for him anyway.

"Cut that out, girls!" shrieked Prissy.

"We don't have time to deal with these silly slayers. We must hurry."

Bruno fell to the ground with a thud. Then he and J.D. ran out of the Fun House as fast as they could go.

Bruno threw his water pistol to Axel. "Here, take this!" he yelled. "I'm not a slayer! I wasn't really going to squirt them with this rosewater. Honest!"

Axel, Thistle, and Wilbur watched in surprise as Bruno and J.D. ran away.

Axel shrugged. He picked up the water pistol and put it in his pocket.

Sissy, Prissy, and Chrissy flew out of the Fun House. Their hair streamed behind them, long and wild.

"Aaahh!" yelled Axel. "It's those vampire brides from Crittervania!"

"Great-Uncle Dracul Duck's really in for it now," gasped Thistle.

"We've got to warn him…before it's too late!" yelled Axel.

Axel, Thistle, and Wilbur ran after the brides toward the main tent.

In the tent, Dracul Duck and Agnes Pinch were centered in the spotlight. "The fango tango, please," Dracul Duck told the bandleader. "Hit it, boys!"

Dracul Duck gracefully twirled Agnes Pinch around and around. His cape billowed as he dipped her all the way to the floor.

The crowd gasped.

Dracul Duck and Agnes Pinch tangoed around the dance floor. The crowd clapped. No one had ever seen dancing like that in Critter Falls before.

Suddenly, the tent was filled with horrible shrieking sounds. The vampire brides flew above the crowd, their eyes glowing red and their fangs gleaming white.

Everyone looked up and screamed.

"There he is!" screamed Prissy. "He's dancing with that old bag!"

"Oh, no!" gasped Wanda. "The brides!"

"They look like they're out for blood," said Jack.

Prissy waved her arms over the crowd. Then she said:

"Lightning and thunder, it is our will,
may the sands of time now stand still!"

Thunder boomed and lightning flashed across the sky.

The citizens of Critter Falls froze in place

as all the clocks in Critter Falls stopped at the stroke of 8:36. Only the brides and the Howls were unfrozen.

The vampire brides headed over to Dracul Duck. "It's not what you think," he whimpered.

"How dare you dance with someone else?" yelled Prissy.

"We're your dancing partners," added Sissy.

"Forever," reminded Chrissy.

Dracul Duck gulped. His eyes widened in fear.

"Now, wait just a minute," began Jack. "You can't tell him what to do. He's his own duck—or should I say, vampire."

"That's right," agreed Wanda. "You can't just fly into town and cause all this trouble. You unfreeze time right this second!"

"You big meanies!" said Thistle.

"Leave Great-Uncle Dracul Duck alone!" yelled Axel.

Sissy, Prissy, and Chrissy just laughed their horrible shrieking laughs.

No one noticed Dracul Duck slip out of the tent.

"What does he see in this sorry excuse for a mortal anyway?" asked Sissy. She turned on Mrs. Pinch. Agnes stood with her arms up in the air and a silly smile on her face.

"Beats me," said Sissy.

"Must be a great dancer," said Chrissy.

"I have an idea," said Prissy. "Let's take her back to Crittervania, to the castle. We'll make her tell us all her secrets."

The three brides laughed evilly.

"Oh, no, you don't!" said Jack Howl.

But it was too late. In a blink, the vampire brides and Mrs. Pinch vanished into thin air...

Coffin Potato

Back at Old Howl Hall, Dracul Duck was in the crypt. He was sitting miserably in his coffin, flipping from channel to channel on the TV. He stared blankly at the screen.

"Relationships dragging you down?" boomed a talk show host on TV. "Stop changing channels! Keep listening. The time to change your life is now!"

"You mean death," said Dracul Duck. He put down the remote control and sat up straighter in his coffin.

"Sometimes you have to put your foot

down," said the talk show host. "And then you have to cut off all those old relationships that no longer work for you! Because you are number  one! Repeat after me. 'I am number one!'"

"I am number one," recited Dracul Duck obediently.

"For starters, stop hanging out with them!" said the talk show host. "Do your own thing! Once you take that first big step, you'll see there's no turning back."

Dracul Duck nodded. "You're right," he said to the TV set. "I left those brides. That's a big step for a vampire like me."

"After you've taken that step, give yourself a big pat on the back," continued the talk show host.

Dracul Duck patted himself on the back.

"Now, you're ready for step two," advised the talk show host. "No more Mr. Nice Guy.

Let your teeth come out. Let them see that you mean business."

Dracul Duck bared his fangs and growled.

Just then, the Howls burst into the crypt.

Wanda turned off the TV set. She stared at Dracul Duck intently. "Dracul Duck, this is important," said Wanda. "You've got to listen to me. It's your castle. And it's your life—or should I say, death—and you have the right to do whatever you want."

"You can't let the brides run the show," added Jack. "You're your own vampire. You've got to stand up to them."

"I can't do it," whined Dracul Duck.

"Yes, you can," said Axel. "Remember, you're the head vampire."

"That's right!" said Thistle.

Dracul Duck stared at the Howls. He thought about the talk show he had just seen. He knew they were right, but the brides would be so angry. There was no telling what they would do.

"You must," encouraged Wanda. "If not for us, then for Mrs. Pinch. We've got to save her, and you've got to help us."

"You're right," said Dracul Duck, getting out of the coffin. "I'll give it a try. But I can't guarantee anything."

"Then it's settled," said Wanda. "We will go to Crittervania. I don't like to do this, but since this is an emergency, it's the only way."

Wanda waved her arms and said:

"Forces of lightning, thunder, and snow, to Crittervania—here we go!"

A flash of lightning lit up the room. The Howls and Dracul Duck disappeared in a puff of smoke.

The Tickle Chamber

Far away in Crittervania, Mrs. Pinch was in the dungeon of Castle Dracul Duck. The vampire brides were gathered around her.

"All right, girls," ordered Prissy. She held up a long peacock feather. "On the count of three, we tickle her." Sissy and Chrissy held their feathers at the ready.

"Please don't tickle me!" wailed Mrs. Pinch. "I'm very ticklish."

"One, two, three," intoned Prissy. "Now—dance, Mrs. Pinch!"

"I hate to dance!" squealed Mrs. Pinch.

"I told you before.
I'm a terrible dancer."

But Sissy, Prissy, and
Chrissy wouldn't listen.
They began to tickle her toes.

"Ha, ha, ha!" laughed Mrs. Pinch. She
jumped up and down as she tried to get
away from the feathers. "Ho, ho, ho! Please
stop!" she gasped. She was laughing so
hard that tears ran down her cheeks.

"Not so fast," said Chrissy.

"Hold your horses, chubby," added Sissy.

Prissy turned to a silver mirror.

"Mirror, mirror, on the wall," said Prissy.
"Who's the best dancer of them all?"

The mirror came to life. "Mrs. Pinch," it
answered. "For the twenty-ninth time."

Sissy, Prissy, and Chrissy all bared their
fangs. They began to growl low in their
throats as they glared at Mrs. Pinch.

Mrs. Pinch screamed in horror. And then
she fell into a dead faint.

"I know," suggested Sissy. "Maybe we should turn her into a vampire."

"Bad idea," said Prissy. "Then there will be four of us."

"Just what we *don't* want," said Chrissy.

Meanwhile, the Howls and Dracul Duck had arrived at the castle and were looking everywhere for Mrs. Pinch.

"I bet I know where she is," said Dracul Duck. "Follow me." He led them down a long curving flight of dusty stone steps to the dungeon.

At the bottom was a heavy wooden door. The Howls peered through the wrought iron bars at the top.

"Oh, no!" gasped Wanda.

Mrs. Pinch was awake. All three brides were shrieking and tickling her again.

Dracul Duck took a deep breath. "I can do it," he mumbled to himself. "Because I am number one."

Without another thought, Dracul Duck

knocked the door down. He charged into the room. Wanda, Jack, Axel, and Thistle were right behind him.

Everyone froze. Silence descended on the dungeon.

"Okay, that's enough!" ordered Dracul Duck. "Let her go!"

"He's back!" screamed Chrissy.

"Isn't that nice!" echoed Sissy.

"But you're too late!" barked Prissy. "Anyway, we give the orders, not you! Now tickle her! I'll take care of them."

Prissy flew up in the air. She was ready to attack the Howls.

"Here!" shouted Axel. "It's rosewater." He threw the water pistol to Dracul Duck.

Dracul Duck pointed the gun at Prissy. Then he squirted her.

"Aaahh!" screamed Prissy as her arm began to burn from the water. "That hurt!"

"How could you do that to her?" yelled Sissy.

"You're so mean!" said Chrissy.

"All right, brides," barked Dracul Duck. "You've overstayed your welcome for centuries. The time to leave is *now!*"

"What?" sputtered all three brides.

"Read my bill!" shouted Dracul Duck. "Scoot! Scram! Get lost! N-O-W—Now!"

"No!" moaned Sissy. "We can't leave!"

"We'll be good vampires!" promised Chrissy.

"We'll do whatever you say," pleaded Prissy.

"Nope," said Dracul Duck firmly. "I'm sorry, but that's the way it is. It's for your own good."

The three brides burst into tears. They sobbed as if their hearts would break.

Wanda, Jack, Axel, and Thistle gathered around Dracul Duck.

"We're so proud of you," beamed Wanda.

"I did what had to be done," said Dracul Duck. "Thanks to all of you."

He smiled at the Howls.

"Now unfreeze time," Dracul Duck ordered Prissy.

Prissy did as Dracul Duck had said. Then she, Sissy, and Chrissy went to pack their bags.

The Howls, Dracul Duck, and Mrs. Pinch got back to the dance contest just as all the clocks in Critter Falls began ticking once again. No one was aware that anything out of the ordinary had happened at all.

The loudspeaker crackled to life. "And the winner of the Critter Falls dance contest is…Mrs. Pinch," announced the band-leader. "And her mysterious stranger."

The crowd clapped. Mrs. Pinch bounced up to the podium to pick up her trophy. She beamed at the audience. "I would like to thank my mysterious stranger, wherever he is!"

Out of the darkness, Dracul Duck glided up to the podium.

The crowd gasped.

Then suddenly, the crowd began to wave their arms at Dracul Duck and shout: "Do the fango tango!"

Dracul Duck nodded at the crowd. Then he turned to the band. "Hit it, boys!"

Everyone lined up behind Dracul Duck.

"Jump to the left and dip to the right," said Dracul Duck as he jumped and then dipped low to the ground.

The crowd did just what he had done.

"Now *bite! bite! bite!*" shouted Dracul Duck, baring his fangs. "Then dip to the left and jump to the right, and *bite! bite! bite!* Then let's fango tango again!"

And that is how the fango tango came to be the most celebrated dance step in all of Critter Falls!

Meanwhile, back in Crittervania, the vampire brides trudged sadly away from Castle Dracul Duck. They headed down the mountain into town.

"What are we going to do?" sighed Sissy.

"Let's stop here for the night," suggested Prissy. She pointed to an inn.

The vampire brides went into the inn. It was crowded with travelers.

"Can I help you?" asked the innkeeper.

"Yes," said Prissy. "We'd like a room for the night."

"Where are you from?" asked the innkeeper.

"Castle Dracul Duck," answered Chrissy.

"Aaahhh!" screamed the innkeeper and all the travelers. They ran out of the inn as fast as they could go.

And that is how the vampire brides came to run a quaint little inn in Crittervania they called the Honeymoon Hotel. You can check in any time you want, but you'll never check out again...